How the
LEOPARD
Got His Spots

For Bosmere's Year 1
Reading Club and Year 3 — all
Shoo Rayner fans!

...d out more about
Rudyard Kipling's
JUST so STORIES

at Shoo Rayner's fabulous website,

www.shoo-rayner.co.uk

First published in 2007 by Orchard Books
First paperback publication in 2008

ORCHARD BOOKS
338 Euston Road, London NW1 3BH
Orchard Books Australia
Level 17/207 Kent St, Sydney, NSW 2000

ISBN 978 1 84616 400 2 (hardback)
ISBN 978 1 84616 409 5 (paperback)

A CIP catalogue record for this book is available from the British Library.

1 3 5 7 9 10 8 6 4 2 (hardback)
1 3 5 7 9 10 8 6 4 2 (paperback)

Printed and bound in England by Antony Rowe Ltd, Chippenham, Wiltshire

Orchard Books is a division of Hachette Children's Books,
an Hachette Livre UK company.

www.orchardbooks.co.uk

Rudyard Kipling's
JUST SO STORIES

How the
LEOPARD
Got His Spots

Retold and illustrated by

SHOO RAYNER

ORCHARD BOOKS

Long, long ago, at the very beginning
of time, when everything was just
getting sorted out, there lived
a Leopard. He was sandy-yellow
and greyish-brown all over.

He lived in a place called the High Veldt, which was all sand and sand-coloured rock and sandy-yellow grass.

The Giraffe and the Zebra
also lived on the High Veldt.
They were sandy-yellow and
greyish-brown all over too,
but the Leopard was the
sandy-yellowest,
greyish-brownest
of them all.

The Leopard matched the colour
of the High Veldt exactly.

So he could lie down behind
a rock or clump of grass, and
surprise the Giraffe and the Zebra
out of their jumpsome lives!

A Man also lived on the High Veldt. He and the Leopard were friends and they often hunted together.

The Man with his bows and arrows,

and the Leopard with his teeth and claws.

Bows and arrows and teeth and claws

Bow-strings are made from woven fibres of the sisal plant.

Bows are made from acacia wood.

Sisal

Acacia

The sharp point is dipped in *deadly poison*!

Arrow flights are made from chicken feathers.

To keep claws in top hunting condition, they need frequent sharpening.

The Giraffe and the Zebra
sneaked away from the Leopard
and the Man. They went to a great
forest, full of trees and bushes and
stripy, speckly, patchy-blatchy
shadows, and there they hid.

After a long time standing under the slippery-slidy shadows of the trees, the Giraffe grew blotchy,

and the Zebra grew stripy. They had a wonderful time in the speckly-spickly forest.

Meanwhile the Leopard and the Man ran all over the yellow, greyish-brown High Veldt, wondering where all their breakfasts and dinners and teas had gone.

They were so hungry they had to eat rats and beetles and rock-rabbits, which gave them terrible tummy-aches.

Things that give you terrible tummy-aches

Deep-fried rat tails can give you the *squiggles*.

Some crunchy beetles can give you the *rumblin' tums*.

Eating too much grass will make you moo!

Moo!

Rocks are tastier than rock-rabbits.

Purple berries are tasty but they can stain your insides out.

One day they met
Baviaan the Baboon, the
wisest animal in all Africa.

"Where have all the animals from the High Veldt gone?" the Leopard asked Baviaan.

Baviaan winked. He knew. "They're in other spots. My advice is to go in other spots too."

15

The Leopard was puzzled, but he and the Man set off looking for other spots. After many days, they came to a great forest all speckled and sprottled and spotted, dotted and splashed and slashed and hatched and cross-hatched with shadows.

"This must be the place," said the Man. "I can smell Giraffe, and I can hear Giraffe, but I can't see Giraffe."

"That's curious," said the Leopard, "because I can smell Zebra, and I can hear Zebra, but I can't see Zebra."

"Perhaps we've forgotten what they look like?" said the Man.

"Nonsense!" said the Leopard. "I remember them perfectly. Giraffe is very tall, and golden-yellow from head to heel. Zebra is not so tall, and a grey-fawn colour from head to heel."

"Hmm," said the Man, looking into the speckly-spickly shadows of the forest. "Then they ought to show up in this dark place like a bunch of ripe bananas."

But the Leopard and the Man hunted
all day, and though they could smell
and hear Giraffe and Zebra, they never
saw them.

"For goodness' sake," said the
Leopard at teatime, "let's wait till it gets
dark. This daylight hunting is getting
us nowhere."

Things you can smell but not see

Marsh Gas
A bit stinky, but you can see it when lightning sets fire to it.

Wildfire
When you smell this, run!

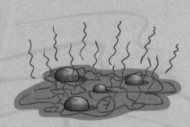

Fear
Animals can smell fear.
It's what makes your hair stand up on end.

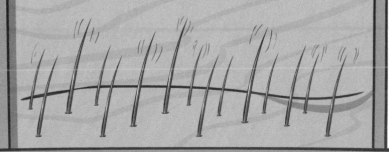

Long after the sun went down, the Leopard heard something breathe all sniffily in the starlight that fell all stripy through the branches.

He jumped on it.

It smelt like Zebra,

and it felt like Zebra,

and when he
knocked it down it
kicked like Zebra.

"Be quiet, you zebra-like thing,"
growled the Leopard. "I am going
to sit on your head till morning,
when I can see you."

"Don't trust it," said the Leopard. "Sit on its head till the morning, same as me."

So they sat down hard till the morning sun rose in the sky.

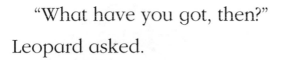

"What have you got, then?"
Leopard asked.

The Man scratched his head, "It
ought to be golden-yellow from head
to heel, and it ought to be Giraffe,
but it's all covered in chestnut
blotches. What have you got?"

The Leopard scratched his head, "It ought to be a greyish-fawn colour, and it ought to be Zebra, but it is covered all over with black stripes. What have you been doing to yourself, Zebra? If you were on the High Veldt I could see you ten miles away!"

"But I'm not on the High Veldt," said the Zebra. "Can't you see?"

"I can see now," said the Leopard. "But I couldn't see you yesterday. How do you do it?"

"Stop sitting on us," said the Zebra, "and we'll show you."

When the Leopard and the Man got up, Zebra scampered away to some thorn-bushes where the sunlight fell all stripy, and Giraffe tripped off to some trees where the shadows fell all blotchy.

"Now watch," said the Zebra and the Giraffe. "This is the way it's done. One–two–three! And where's your breakfast now?"

Leopard stared,

and Man stared,
but the Zebra and
the Giraffe had
disappeared into
the shadowy forest.

37

"Now that's a trick worth learning," said the Man. "You don't match your background any more, Leopard. Take Baviaan's advice and go into spots."

"What's the use of that?" said the Leopard.

"Think of Giraffe," said the Man, "or if you prefer stripes, think of Zebra. Their spots and stripes blend in perfectly."

"Hmm," said the Leopard. "I don't want to look like Zebra."

"Well, make up your mind," said the Man, "because I'd hate to go hunting without you, but I must if you insist on standing out like a sunflower."

"I'll take spots, then," said the Leopard. "Not too big – I don't want to look like Giraffe."

"I'll make them with
the tips of my fingers,"
said the Man.

41

The Man picked
a handful of berries
and squeezed out the
blackish-brown juice.

He dipped his fingers in the juice,
and pressed them all over the Leopard.
Wherever his fingers touched they left
five little marks close together. You
can see them on any Leopard you like.

"Now!" said the Man, "You can lie on the ground and look like a heap of pebbles,

or lie on the rocks and look like a piece of stone.

"You can lie on a leafy branch and look like sunshine through the leaves, and you can lie across the centre of a path and look like nothing in particular. Think of that!"

"But if I'm all this," said the Leopard, "why don't you go spotty too?"

45

The man smeared dark hunting stripes across his face. "Oh, I hunt better by hiding in the shadows with my bows and arrows. Now come along and we'll see if we can't get even with

Mr One-Two-Three-Where's-Your-Breakfast!"

So they went away and they lived happily ever after.

And the Leopard has never changed his spots again because he is quite contented as he is.

Rudyard Kipling's JUST SO STORIES

Retold and illustrated by

SHOO RAYNER

All priced at £8.99

Rudyard Kipling's Just So Stories are available from all good bookshops,
or can be ordered direct from
the publisher: Orchard Books, PO BOX 29, Douglas IM99 1BQ
Credit card orders please telephone 01624 836000
or fax 01624 837033 or visit our internet site: www.orchardbooks.co.uk
or e-mail: bookshop@enterprise.net for details.

To order please quote title, author and ISBN
and your full name and address.
Cheques and postal orders should be made payable to 'Bookpost plc.'
Postage and packing is FREE within the UK
(overseas customers should add £2.00 per book).

Prices and availability are subject to change.

So they went away and they lived happily ever after.

And the Leopard has never changed his spots again because he is quite contented as he is.

Rudyard Kipling's JUST SO STORIES

Retold and illustrated by
SHOO RAYNER

All priced at £8.99

Rudyard Kipling's Just So Stories are available from all good bookshops,
or can be ordered direct from
the publisher: Orchard Books, PO BOX 29, Douglas IM99 1BQ
Credit card orders please telephone 01624 836000
or fax 01624 837033 or visit our internet site: www.orchardbooks.co.uk
or e-mail: bookshop@enterprise.net for details.

To order please quote title, author and ISBN
and your full name and address.
Cheques and postal orders should be made payable to 'Bookpost plc.'
Postage and packing is FREE within the UK
(overseas customers should add £2.00 per book).

Prices and availability are subject to change.